George Rose

Heart and Harp

A Book of Lyrics

George Rose

Heart and Harp
A Book of Lyrics

ISBN/EAN: 9783744787727

Printed in Europe, USA, Canada, Australia, Japan

Cover: Foto ©Andreas Hilbeck / pixelio.de

More available books at **www.hansebooks.com**

HEART AND HARP

A BOOK OF LYRICS

BY

' GEORGE ROSE.

THE MADISON SQUARE PRESS,
H. H. B. ANGELL, PUBLISHER,
354 Fourth Avenue,
New York,

Lovingly,

In memory of

MY MOTHER,

and respectfully,

In regard of my honored friend

MRS. ISABELLE MONTAGUE GEER,

this collection of my verses

is inscribed.

PREFACE.

WITH but few exceptions the poems appearing in this little volume have already been published; many of them in the "Churchman," and the "New York Observer."

The Easter Carol, "Jesus, Prince of Loveland," was written for the Infant Classes of Saint Timothy's Church, New York City; teachers, Miss Fanny J. Gibson and Miss Hilda Marshall. Excellent music for it has been composed by Mr. Chas. H. Sunderland, the talented and esteemed organist of the church.

To George William Warren, Mus, Doc., I am indebted for music for the Easter Carol: "A Song of Sweetness," which has been sung repeatedly with gratifying effect at Saint Thomas' Church, under Dr. Warren's able direction.

With the hope and trust that something in this book will be found worthy the reader's thoughtful attention, "Heart and Harp" is launched, with all modesty, upon the vasty sea of literature.

THE AUTHOR.

New York, October, 1887,

CONTENTS.

CATHEDRAL OF SAINT JOHN THE DIVINE, NEW YORK.

Thou didst the lofty theme inspire,
　　Sweet Muse ; the flowing song attend,
　　That men the listening ear may bend ;
O touch my harp with heavenly fire !

A time to build ! lo, halcyon Peace,
　　Of smiling face and gracious hand,
　　Is sovereign in all the land,
Where boundless riches aye increase.

A time our wealth to consecrate
　　To God of never ending days ;
　　The Deity benign to praise
In manner glorious and great.

A time for Him the stone to mould,
　　And give it semblance rich and rare ;
　　To set it living in the air,
Fresh strength and beauty to unfold.

A time His name to magnify
   With windows of a gorgeous hue,
   Our adoration to renew
When we in dust and ashes lie.

A time, indeed, to grow the flow'r
   Resplendent of the century,
   That shall o'er us, unconsciously,
Exert a high and holy pow'r.

A time to bid the landmark rise,
   The nations of the earth to guide ;
   Two neighb'ring countries to divide ;
But one is veiled from mortal eyes.

A time the beacon to uprear,
   T' illuminate the occident ;
   To light afar the orient,
That mariners to port may steer.

A time from worldly things to soar ;
   To cleave the welkin like the dove ;
   To look beyond us and above,
E'en in the task sublime before.

A goodly spectacle to see !
   Imposed upon the lordly base,
   The sign of a redeemèd race—
The Cross of Christianity.

FROM A FOREIGN SHORE.

AN explosion at the mouth of a coal mine in Saxony, conveyed to a number of colliers within, that before many minutes they would be in another world. Confronting death in the gas slowly approaching them, how calmly they met it the loving and pious messages told, that were written to friends and relatives upon scraps of paper or in note-books, which were afterward found upon their bodies. One read, "*No more toil in darkness.*"

LETTERS, friends ! letters from over the seas !
   Here they are—kiss them and kiss them again ;
   Telling of wonders beyond all our ken—
Endlessly blossoming flowers and trees,
Odorous evergreen pastures and leas,
   Streamlets and rivers of glittering gold,
   Hamlets and cities of beauty untold ;
Gorgeous of sunlight and blissful of ease—
Letters, friends ! letters from over the seas !

Letters, friends ! letters from over the seas !
   Ay, from a fair and a far away land
   Something once pressed by the dear one's sweet
      hand ;
Ready, good minister ! read them now please,
We are uncovered and down on our knees ;
   Hark ye ! good tidings from every one,
   Husband and brother and father and son ;
Letters—O praise and thanksgiving for these !
Soundeth *all's well!*—and from over the seas.

THE OLD YEAR.

SAD wreck upon the waves of time,
Dark driftwood of an Arctic clime,
Only of failure great, sublime ;
    Avaunt, Old year ! avaunt !

Where is the treasure promised me ?
Down at the bottom of the sea !
Hence ! ghost of what thou wast to be ;
    Old year, avaunt ! avaunt !

THE NEW YEAR.

GOD bless the day ! a sail ! there—there !
It seemeth as a vision fair :
What spotlessness ! what beauty rare !—
    All hail, New Year ! all hail !

Scudding beneath a cloudless sky,
Whilst billows hymn a symphony,
Behold ! my golden argosy :
    New Year, all hail ! all hail !

IN MEMORIAM.

The Rev. George Jarvis Geer, D. D.

The summons " Higher ! " sounds again ;
　And, hark ! the answer—" Waiting, Lord ! "
　And, lo, the talents ten* restored
With usury—e'en other ten.

Think ye, the host seraphic came
　To quench the light ? its mission done
　Below, full rounded as the sun
It rose on high—a deathless flame !

This flow'r which in affection grew,
　I drop, with many a falling tear,
　Upon thy rose-embowered bier,
My faithful friend and pastor true.

'Tis hushed ! the fond, entreating voice,
　So resonant of tender love,
　Beseeching e'er the One above—
" O, feed thy lambs with verdure choice."

---

* In the parable there are but five talents ; the writer, however, found the number ten more available for rhyme in this instance.

'Tis stilled ! the hand both brave and bold,
　Which guided wanderers astray
　Into the peaceful, perfect way ;
And kept the wolves without the fold.

'Tis dimmed ! the bright, benignant eye,
　That, to th' unsullied waterbrook,
　With earnest gaze and steadfast look,
Constrained the flock, how tenderly !

Alas, the wailing far and wide ;
　The sheep are looking round in vain
　For one who will not come again ;
His arms have fallen by his side.

Yet speaketh he as ne'er before ;
　His touch is warm ; his smile they see :
　Yea, doubly and unceasingly
His charge beloved he watcheth o'er.

They are not comfortless ; for HE,
　The gracious Shepherd over all,
　Doth now how plainly, loudly call
Across the moorland—" Follow me ! "

A SERMON FROM BRUSSELS.

In Brussels bright upon the town-hall's ceiling,
 A form is pictured marvelous to see ;
Intently I behold it with the feeling
 That calmly it is peering down on me.

To right I go—and, then, to left--amazing !
 Upon me ever rest the life-like eyes ;
Far off I stand, and, steadfastly there gazing,
 I view them still with infinite surprise.

To-day in Europe but away to-morrow,
 When all forgotten may yon wonder be ;
But, O, the lesson from it I may borrow,
 Is worth a pilgrimage across the sea.

Above there are e'en' other eyes all-seeing,
 Which follow after every way I turn ;
In sweetness, grace, and majesty, agreeing,
 That mine eyes some day shall unveiled discern.

A FABLE.

As joined him on his winding way,
  Fair tributary waters ;
The Mississippi cried one day—
  " A husband for my daughters !
Both rich and gen'rous he must be ;
  For they must lack, O, never ! "
Then all to Neptune married he—
  Forever and forever.

Ho, from the speeding torrent learn
  A lesson aye inviting ;
The days of nuptials will return,
  The man and maid uniting :
But whom to wed ? why, marry—Love,
  That deep than ocean greater ;
So shall we true to nature prove,
  And nature's wise Creator.

EASTER CAROL : "A SONG OF SWEETNESS."

A SONG of sweetness fills the air,
From bounding Nature smiling fair ;
      This joyful morn !
The flowers gaily blossoming,
In chorus swelling softly sing ;
      New born ! new born !

The budding brakes and blooming trees,
Are framing choice antiphonies ;
      This joyful morn !
The hills and mountains verdure clad,
Attuned awake the accents glad ;
      New born ! new born !

No longer bound by winter's cold,
Adown the stream the music's rolled ;
      This joyful morn !
Redeemed—'t is meet that man should raise
The rarest canticle of praise ;
      New born ! new born !

Why, then, rejoice ! acclaim the lay !
All things begin anew to-day ;
       'T is Easter morn !
Hail ! celebrate O earth ! O sky !
O'er hateful death—the victory :
       New born ! new born !

———

RISING : A LEGEND OF EASTER.

List, friends ! before the cross one day
A magdalen did meekly pray ;
And falling fast her tear-drops lay
    Upon the blood-stains there :

(And yet, like April's weeping sky,
That briny stream saith--spring is nigh,
When birds discourse and suddenly
    Appear the blossoms fair :)

The spots—the crimson spots became
E'en fresh, and dripped once more ; " The blame
Is mine," she cried ; " O, shame ! O, shame !
    That I such guilt should bear ! "

But, lo, the change ! unsoiled of blood,
The tree before the woman stood ;
Bathed in the sunshine's golden flood,
    And decked of roses rare :

And, then, the feathered tribe did pour
What songs abroad ! and o'er and o'er
She smiled—who never smiled before ;
    Her heart as light as air :

The tale is told.—'T is said e'er bright
Remained the flowers to her sight ;
And giving her, O, what delight !
    Their scent was everywhere.

GOD'S ACRE.

"Dust to dust." July 8th, 1884.

I.

The depths perturbed—yet all is well;
The heavens surcharged—but who can tell
The joy of rest, the bliss of peace,
Succeeding e'er the storm's surcease.

II.

Here many come constrained of woe,
And others come who never go ;
Yet all who mourn departed friends
At last shall come where mourning ends.

III.

With arms about her offspring dear,
Again in accents sweet and clear,
Our best of mothers, Nature, saith—
" I cherish unto life, not death."

IV.

A paradox ! the never mute
Is found in silence absolute ;
Melodious as ocean's waves,
There 's naught so full of speech as graves.

V.

Awaiting harvest ! O, what rare,
Surpassing wealth these furrows bear ;
And, O, when He shall hither come,
What tongue shall sing the harvest-home !

VI.

Now Knowledge crieth from the grave,
"Heed ye, who lore excelling crave ;
This to the wise the wise doth give—
'Here learn the while ye live, to live.' "

THE OLD CHURCH.

This house of worship—is it plain ?
　　Yet is it hallowèd and dear !
　　Associations cluster here,
Whose mem'ry shall undimm'd remain.

'T is not the temple's tow'ring height,
　　Nor yet its store of sculptur'd stone,
　　That maketh rich : 't is this alone—
The Holy Spirit's treasure bright.

These walls bespeak protecting care ;
　　In stormy days they firm did prove :
　　Uprear'd of faith and hope and love,
They 're eloquent of praise and prayer.

When time at last shall cast them down,
　　Of beauty luring to the eye,
　　May others here then typify—
" Above the Cross, behold, the Crown !"

THE NEW CHURCH.

Prepare the temple for your King ;
   Construct the holy fane ;
Know that to God an offering
   Is never made in vain :
He saith, whose promise faileth ne'er—
   " Lo, where my name I write,
I will abide in glory there
   By day, and yet, by night."

To Him, then, the exalted One,
   Upbuild with royal will ;
And evermore the sweet " Well-done ! "
   His earthly house shall fill :
With labor here the workmen lay
   Foundations broad and true,
That, yonder, all amazed they may
   Rare superstructures view.

MAGIC.

For her—a single, simple rose !
　Unworthy 't is my queen I know ;
As lovely, many another grows ;
　Full modest is the tribute so.

But, see ! it decks her bosom fair ;
　Ah, now the trifle sweet, behold !
How pure ! what grace beyond compare !
　'T is worth Golconda's store of gold.

Thus—thus she changes everything ;
　Lo, by the treasures bright of earth,
She deigned to take mine offering,
　And gave it so e'en priceless worth.

O lady dear ! O precious flower—
　That seemed for her a gift how small !
Yet love has aye the wondrous power
　Of making little—all in all.

THE BURIAL OF BISHOP POTTER.

BISHOP HORATIO POTTER was laid to rest clad in his robes of office. "Jerusalem, the Golden," was sung at his grave, and before the earth closed over him his coffin was strewed with violets.

His peaceful couch with flowers strew,
As o'er the slopes the winds breathe low—
    Lay him down,
    Lay him down !
All, all as spotless as the snow,
    Lay him down !

With folded hands upon his breast,
In flowing, meet apparel drest,
    Lay him down,
    Lay him down !
To undisturbed and balmy rest,
    Lay him down !

As saints attending from above
Among the living softly move,
    Lay him down,
    Lay him down !
The while we sing of Light and Love,
    Lay him down !

Fear not ! the angels watch will keep,
Till HE the golden sheaves shall reap ;
　　　Lay him down,
　　　Lay him down !
E'en like a happy child to sleep,
　　　Lay him down !

———

CONFIRMATION.

A MEMORY OF BISHOP HORATIO POTTER.

THE shepherd of our souls is here ;
　　And, tho' with age his voice is weak,
　　He with what earnestness doth speak !
And, ay, with eloquence sincere :
　　　" Thine for ever ! "

A priest of pow'r ! his office great
　　He filleth to a nicety ;
　　No danger to the church I see
As him I hear ejaculate—
　　　" Thine for ever ! "

Impressive, strong of dignity,
　Erect, upturn'd his eyes
　　Upon the joys of paradise ;
He saith—and O, so let it be—
　　　" Thine for ever ! "

Sweet memory ! the other day,
　As down he laid his head to rest
　　Upon that other Shepherd's breast,
Far off I heard the bishop say—
　　　" *Mine for ever !* "
—*St. Timothy's.*

WESTMINSTER ABBEY.

AN ever-changing eager throng,
　From worlds both old and new ;
But, grouped in shadow, who are they—
　All wondering I view ?

Distinct of form, yet, motionless,
　'Neath arch and column old,
In purple and in ermine dressed,
　Lo, Kings and Queens, behold !

And, they, the trusty Premiers there,
  In flowing robes of state ;
How grand of look ! how grave of mien !
  Those " iron men of fate."

And, near the throne, rare spectacle !
  Intent on things above,
Renowned Defenders of the Faith
  Uphold the Book of Love.

And, yonder, of the eagle eye,
  With truncheon in the hand ;
Are Albion's intrepid Knights,
  Born armies to command.

And, here and there, like chosen links
  Uniting kind to kind,
Are other Monarchs ; theirs the realm
  Of dominating mind.

A host—a host most glorious,
  Before the storied wall ;
And " Lofty Purpose " see ! is stamped
  Upon the brow of all.

An ever-changing, eager throng,
  From worlds both old and new ;
But these—are e'en the mighty dead,
  Recalled of fame to view.

MOTHER GOOSE: "AS DOWNWARD FROM THE TREE TOPS."

As downward from the tree-tops
  At dusk the fays descend,
The night in rout and revel
  Upon the green to spend ;
Then out from holes and crannies
  The elves and brownies prance,
And crying, "Hands together all !"
  Around the toad-stools dance.

Thro' thickets now the beetles
  Their wives and daughters bring,
In search of trusty cobwebs
  To give them each a swing ;
Just as the gnats and millers
  Upon the window knock
And say, "Please ma'am ! may I come in
  And wind the kitchen clock ?"

And as the Liliputians
  Go marching cross the floor,
The curtains round the baby,
  And casement-shades, to draw ;
'Tis time that Claude and Clara
  To bed should softly creep,
To snuggle there like children mice
  And think themselves to sleep.

EASTER CAROL :

"JESUS, PRINCE OF LOVELAND."

Jesus, Prince of Loveland,
  Once a mother's joy,
Innocent and comely
  From a little boy ;
Killed by Roman soldiers,
  Him they buried then ;
But, O, wondrous story !
  He arose again.

    Hail, the budding flowers !
      Hail, the birds of spring !
    Everywhere now telling,
      Christ the Lord is king !

From that happy morning,
  Flowers ne'er so gay,
Everywhere appearing
  Gem the earth this day ;
And in many a carol
  Never half so sweet,
All the birds rejoicing
  Easter dawning greet.
      Hail, the budding flowers ! etc.

If we truly love Him
  We above shall go,
Where unfading flowers
  All unrivalled grow ;
And our voices joining
  We shall joyous sing,
Brighter, sweeter carols
  Than the birds of spring.
      Hail, the budding flowers ! etc.

THE EASTER CROSS.

A Reminiscence of "The Little Church."
Miss F. H., Miss G. G. and Miss F. T., *Altar Committee.*

I.

Where once HE hung upon the nail,
Whilst women near did weep and wail—
Now lillies droop, begonias trail,
    And roses are entwined :

II.

Ay, love it was that hither bore
This treasure sweet in lavish store ;
Bedeckt it all the cross—and more ;
    It there itself enshrined.

LOVE AND DEATH.

Written on the occasion of the illness and partial recovery of
General Grant, May, 1885.

" A LITTLE while !" and yet "a little while !"
Thus Love the King of Terrors did beguile ;
Did thus beguile unweary o'er and o'er,
Till she at length beguiled him from the door.

THE GRAVE OF THE CHRISTIAN SOLDIER.

STAND here—but not to mourn,
  Beside the soldier's tomb,
Where bright thro' every chance and change
  Perennial flowers bloom;
The laurel's leaves shall fall
  And moulder in the glade,
But on this grave a chaplet rests
  That time can never fade.

The last farewell is said,
  The conflict fierce is o'er,
And peace beneficent hath come
  To reign forevermore;
The sword is in its sheath,
  The armor is laid down,
And, lo, upon the victor's brow
  Appears the lustrous crown!

LINES TO AN AMERICAN QUEEN.

'TIS meet when queens *live* poetry,
　That laureates attune the lyre ;
'Tis sweet to trumpet royalty
　When gracious deeds the act inspire.

I hold, within the heart 'tis right
　To have enshrined one's sov'reign there ;
He is, methinks, no carpet knight
　Who in his breast his liege doth wear.

Let churls refuse the homage due
　The peerless crown of ladyhood,
But as for me—with rev'rence true
　I bend to it, by all that's good !

A toast ! I drink the debt we owe
　At Beauty's feet—at Virtue's throne ;
The good we worship, we shall know,
　Becometh somehow e'en our own.

SAINT BARTHOLOMEW'S BELL.

THE signal for the massacre of the Huguenots was sounded from the Church of Saint Germain, l'Auxerrois, Paris.

HARK, hark Saint Germain's bell ;
   It crieth on the air—
   Kill, murder everywhere ;
* Nor once of pity tell !

Hark, hark Saint Germain's bell,
   In yonder steeple high
   That pointeth to the sky
Where love and mercy dwell !

Hark, hark Saint Germain's bell ;
   Its rumbling echoes fierce
   The very marrow pierce ;
Deep down they come from hell !

Hark, hark Saint Germain's bell ;
   See, neighbors good and true,
   Here's Guise's bloody crew ;
Our turn has come—farewell !

---

* " That none remain to reproach me."—*Charles IX.*

REFLECTIONS IN A COUNTRY CHURCH.

Not more within the minster tall
    Which opulence for Him provides,
Than in the chapel rude and small—
    The Priest of priests abides.

Perchance before the abbey fine
    The Lord esteems the lowly fane;
Mayhap about the wayside shrine
    His gifts descend like rain.

Fairer than structure reared of hand,
    Within, the pure in heart upraise
The sanctuary—that shall stand
    Beyond the end of days.

THE CHURCH.

STAY ! pilgrim, stay !
  Without how dark the night
No moon doth show her ray,
  Nor any star give light :
The road how wild and drear,
  The rocks how rough and steep,
The precipice how near,
  The stream how broad and deep !
Upon the right or left
  None, none there is to save :
Of reason all bereft,
  Oh, dare not then the wave.
    Stay ! pilgrim, stay !
    Thou must not answer—nay !

Stay ! pilgrim, stay !
  It is the King's behest !
Go not upon thy way,
  But be His royal guest :

Here's water for thy feet,
  And oil to noint thy head ;
And linen fair and sweet,
  And here the table spread :
O make thee here thy home
  Where none have ever died ;
And when thou seest HIM come
  Thou shalt be "satisfied !"
    Stay ! pilgrim, stay !
    Abide, abide for aye !

"BELLE."

"I HAVE had many blessings, but the greatest of earthly joys
has been the love of this dear wife."—*The Rector*.

O SING ye stars ! she loveth me,
  My queenly love whom I love well ;
  The joyous everywhere, O, tell,
Ye tuneful spheres—my ecstacy !

O sing ye stars ! she true will be ;
  To all the leal proclaim her love :
  Voice, everliving worlds above—
My faith in my love's constancy.

HOTEL DIEU.

"WHEN we go where there is suffering we go where something really is."—*Charles Dickens.*

THE house of tears, the halls of pain,
The aisles where fear and terror reign,
The couches rude of misery,
O'erburdened with humanity !
From life's contending hardships free—
You who have wealth and luxury,
You who in cushioned ease rejoice—
Come, with your flow'rs and dainties choice,
Come, with your love and pity sweet,
Lo, where the rich and poor may meet ;
Where all distinctions fade away ;
Come ! change the weary night to day,
E'en by the sunlight of your face :
For Jesus sake *come* to the place—
  "Where something really is ! "

FAME.

WHAT ho, there, rustics ! look ye
   What yonder towers high—
Aladdin's peerless palace—
   Enchanting every eye.

I trow ye marvel, grov'llers !
   " How ever came it there ?"
Then gather, softly, whisper—
   It built upon the air.

The empyrean boldly
   It pierces far away ;
Where proudly now 'tis boasting
   " I come ! and ay, to stay !"

But wherefore, lusty croakers,
   As zephyrs cross the town,
" I told you so !" exclaim ye ?
   Why, zounds !! the castle 's down !

Ho ! tarry, there, ye rustics !
   (A puff—so—and it broke ;)
By all the world's upbuilding,
   It was—ha, ha ! but SMOKE.

PETER VISCHER—WORKMAN.

PETER VISCHER, sculptor and founder, A. D. 1460—1530, executed, among other works, a bronze monument, marvelous in detail and of exquisite beauty, in memory of Saint Sebald ; and which was erected in the church of that name, at Nuremberg. Unmarred of the tooth of time, it remains as it left the hands of the workman.

I.

PETER VISCHER said one day,
"Shall I fritter life away,
And at last repining say—
    Nothing have I done ?"

II.

Peter Vischer workman true,
As good workmen ever do,
Loved his craft and dearly, too ;
    Loved it as his life !

III.

Peter Vischer into art
Wrought his blood and brain and heart ;
And the work in whole and part,
    Lo, was Peter's self !

IV.

Peter Vischer ! is he dead—
Some one near me so hath said ?
Saith the bronze he fashionèd—
" *Vischer liveth still !* "

THE INCARNATION.

O LOOK ye the angels above,
Flying hither and yon like the dove ;
 The Cherubim fair
 Crowned with shimmering hair,
And the Seraphim beaming of love.

O see ye the heralds bedight,
Clad in raiment of glistering white ;
 And marv'lous of mould
 See their trumpets of gold,
Hung with banners refulgent as light.

O wonderment, wonderment, cry ;
They are swinging the censers on high ;
 And th' incense afar
 Streameth down to a star
Which excelleth the host of the sky.

Now list ye with ecstacy meet
What the heights and the heights, yet, repeat ;
   And list with rapt ear
   The refrain sounding clear
In an ultimate antiphon sweet.

SONG OF THE ANGELS.

" Sing - God unto man reconciled !
Lo, the exquisite temple defiled,
   The Christ shall restore
   Unto glory once more ;
Hail, the Virgin's ineffable Child!
          Alleluia !"

"YES!"

O, REDBREAST! gentle robin,
 Of quick, attentive ear;
Say, *didst* thou hear it? *didst* thou—
 That boldly ventured hear?
Why, so thou *didst*, true songster!
 For now, enchanting bird,
To me, and all the forest,
 Thou echoest—one word.

As there your lovely bosoms
 Suffused with blushes swell,
Ye nodding, smiling roses,
 I hearken, what ye tell:
And, pure and spotless lilies,
 With heads depending low,
What modestly ye whisper,
 There's one, full well, doth know!

Above me overspreading,
 Ye bowing, tell-tale trees,
All hail, what ye are giving
 To every passing breeze:

And, as ye lift your voices
  This morning fair and sweet,
Your fond discourse is fathomed,
  O, grass-blades at my feet !

Sing on ! thou feathered minstrel,
  Ye fragrant flowers gay,
Umbrag'ous bow'r, and greensward—
  Prolong your tuneful lay :
I prithee, festive chorus—
  (In any word before
I never heard such music ;)
  Say " *Yes!* " forevermore.

THE "BLACK WATCH:"

Fife and drum !
Fife and drum !
Hark ! in the distance the veterans come !
Hie to the balcony, window and pave,
Proudly to gaze on the spectacle brave ;
Fife and drum,
Fair as the morning the veterans come !

Fife and drum !
Fife and drum !

Banners a-flying the veterans come :
Bayonets flashing like rivers of light,
Moving together now left—and now right,
Fife and drum,
Nearer and nearer the veterans come !

Fife and drum !
Fife and drum !

Eyes straight before them the veterans come !
Yonder is "Shamus"—there's "Sandy"—there's
"Ben !"
Bravest of soldiers and truest of men :
Fife and drum,
Ready now—three cheers ! the veterans come :
Hurrah ! hurrah ! hurrah !

—*London.*

GOOD-NIGHT.

"ENTERED into rest, M. A. at fourscore, at midnight Dec. 31st, 1886."—*Letter*.

UPON the hearth the fire is low,
But here and there the embers glow ;
No heat the crannied house doth warm,
Yet hark ! the wild, contending storm.

About the board went round what cheer,
When first the flame was kindled here ;
And, as it rose and roared with glee,
How merry grew the company !

Hist, hist ! a thief is in the room ;
But where—in all the gath'ring gloom ?
So heavy is the air, and chill,
Congealèd is both brain and will.

'Tis growing dark—how stilly dark !
Remaineth now a single spark ;
There ! *quenched* the sweet, surpassing light,
Please God—the fire is out. Good-night !

THE END.